Naughty Fish

"Coloured Bedtime StoryBook"

By

Mingmala Norlady

Illustrated by

Anyxay Phimmachack

ILLUSTRATED & PUBLISHED
BY
E-KİTAP PROJESİ & CHEAPEST BOOKS

www.cheapestboooks.com

 www.facebook.com/EKitapProjesi

ISBN: 978-625-6308-95-4

Copyright, 2024 by e-Kitap Projesi

Istanbul

Categories: Problem Solving & Animals
Country of Origin: Laos Republic
Cover: © Cheapest Books
License: CC-BY-4.0

For full terms of use and attribution, http://creativecommons.org/licenses/by/4.0/

Contributing: Anyxay Phimmachack

© **All rights reserved.**

Except for the conditions stated in the License, no part of this book shall be reproduced or transmitted in any form or by any means, electronic or mechanical, including photocopy, recording or by any information or retrieval system, without written permission form the publisher.

About the Book

Naughty Fish bullies the small fishes, but one day he needs help. Will the small fishes come to his rescue?

Naughty Fish
Mingmala Norlady
Anyxay Phimmachack

Many animals lived in a clean pond.

There were many fish that swam in the pond.

All of the animals lived happily and peacefully. Until...!

The big fish swam by and caused a disruption. The other fishes named him the Naughty Fish.

The Naughty Fish liked to use his long fish tail to splash water at the other fish.

The Naughty Fish laughed and made fun of the small fishes.

Apart from making fun, the Naughty fish liked to chase...

And fight the small fishes for food.

Each time they saw the Naughty Fish, all of the small fishes would swim away and none of them would want to play with him.

The Naughty Fish was pleased that all of the fishes were scared of him.

One day there was a big storm and heavy rains caused the water level to rise.
The storm washed away the currents. All of the animals became scared and looked for a safe hiding place.

While the Naughty Fish was swimming alone, he got washed away by a strong current.

His tail got caught in a rock. He tried to escape, but he could not.

He was stuck there for many hours.

As the storm came to a halt, all of the animals went back to their homes and helped each other.

On their way home, the small fishes saw the Naughty Fish stuck in the rock. The small fishes wanted to help him, but they had to call on their friends to come help.

The small fishes gathered their friends and explained how to help the Naughty Fish. The small fishes talked among themselves, "He is a naughty fish. Should we help him?"

At last, the small fishes decided to help the Naughty Fish.

The Naughty Fish felt grateful to everyone. When he returned home, he felt bad that he has bullied the others.

Early the next day, the Naughty Fish swam to his friends, but this time he brought them food to share.

Since then, the Naughty Fish has become friends with the other animals and was never called the Naughty Fish again.

End of the Story

www.ingramcontent.com/pod-product-compliance
Lightning Source LLC
LaVergne TN
LVHW070453080526
838202LV00035B/2823